By
Sarah
Ellis

Illustrated by
Dušan
Petričić

THE QUEEN'S FEET

Red Deer Press

Once there was a queen called Queen Daisy who had a great deal of trouble with her feet. Those feet did not want to behave themselves in a royal way at all.

Those feet did not want to wear proper queen shoes. Sometimes, they wanted to wear big yellow gumboots or fuzzy red slippers with faces.

Sometimes, they wanted to wear heavy boots to crash up and down stairs or rubber thongs that flip-flopped when they walked.

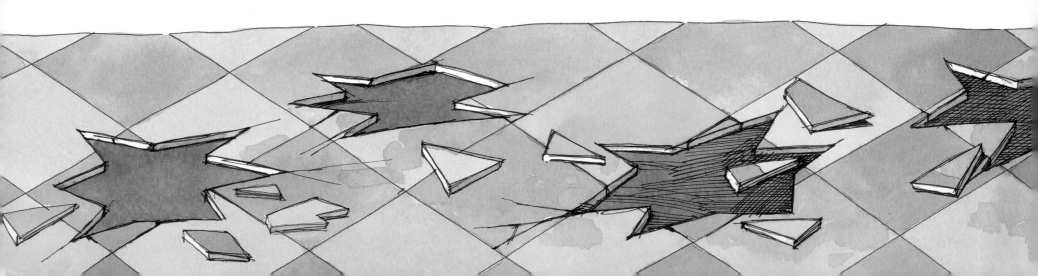

Sometimes, they wanted to wear sandals to show off the queen's special striped socks or her purple painted toenails.

Sometimes, those feet didn't want to wear any shoes at all.

Even when Queen Daisy forced her feet to dress properly, they would not act properly. One day, when she was christening a new ship, those feet made her climb right up the rigging to the crow's nest and dance the hornpipe.

Another time, during a very long speech at a royal dinner, the queen's feet took her down to the kitchen and kept her there telling knock-knock jokes to the cook until all the important people went home.

Once Queen Daisy had to be polite to a whole garden full of ladies in large hats. That day the royal feet made the queen walk right out of her shoes and right into a pond where the goldfish tickled her toes.

The queen's feet were particularly naughty at balls.

They would suddenly begin
kickboxing or doing the splits or
tap-dancing on the marble palace floors.

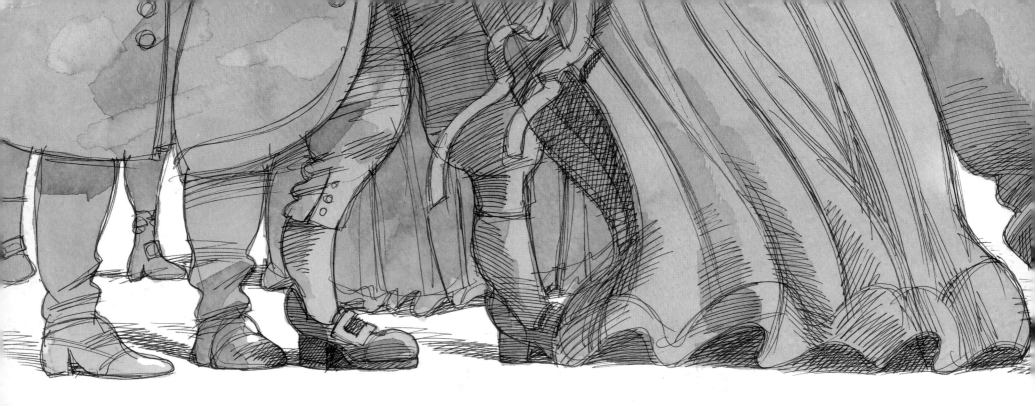

One day the queen's feet went too far.
King Marvin was visiting from a next-door kingdom. He was mean. He was a bully. He thought he was the boss of everybody. The queen's feet felt as though they were being stepped on.

Finally they could not stand it
another minute and one of them kicked the
king in the ankle. They were wearing hiking boots
that day and King Marvin went home very angry.

Queen Daisy wrote a long letter in her best printing to say she was very sorry for the bad behavior of her feet. But her people said,

"Your majesty, it is not enough. Something must be done about those feet, once and for all."

So the queen and the queen's feet invited all the sages, wise women, wizards, fairy godmothers, and, of course, footmen, in the land to a meeting.

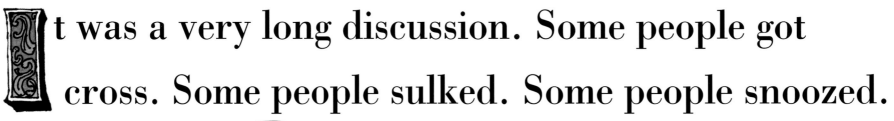

It was a very long discussion. Some people got cross. Some people sulked. Some people snoozed.

And everyone's feet got very restless.

But, finally, they sorted it out. The queen's feet agreed to behave royally most of the time. They would wear proper shoes, walk quietly, dance sedately, and stay out of puddles.

But for one hour each day, the hour when afternoon slips into evening, the queen's feet could be footloose and fancy-free. They could cut up, act out, and carry on. They could raise a ruckus and kick up a fuss.

For one hour each day the queen's feet ruled.

From that time on, the only trouble Queen Daisy had with her feet was that sometimes after a day of presentations and proclamations they got tired. When that happened she would stay home in the evening and share a lemon popsicle with her husband, Prince Fred. He would give her feet a good rub. And that was very nice. For both of them.

Northern Lights Books for Children are published by Red Deer Press
A Fitzhenry & Whiteside Company
1512, 1800–4 Street S.W., Calgary, Alberta, Canada T2S 2S5
www.reddeerpress.com

Credits
Edited for the Press by Peter Carver
Design by Blair Kerrigan/Glyphics
Printed and bound in China by Paramount Book Art for Red Deer Press

Acknowledgments
Financial support provided by the Canada Council, the Government of Canada through the Book Publishing Industry Development Program (BPIDP).

THE CANADA COUNCIL | LE CONSEIL DES ARTS
FOR THE ARTS | DU CANADA
SINCE 1957 | DEPUIS 1957

National Library of Canada Cataloguing in Publication

Ellis, Sarah
The queen's feet / Sarah Ellis ; illustrated by Dušan Petričić.

(Northern lights books for children)
ISBN 0-88995-320-1

I. Petričić, Dušan II. Title. III. Series.
PS8559.L57Q43 2005   jC813'.6   C2005-904194-3

5 4 3 2 1

The illustrations in *The Queen's Feet* were done in Ecoline watercolor and pen and ink.

For Karl and Sheila
— Sarah Ellis

For Katarina, my smiling granddaughter.
— Dušan Petričić